BIG HAIR, DON'T CARE

Goldest Karat Publishing

340 S Lemon Ave #1077

Walnut, CA 91789

Find more books like this at www.goldestkarat.com.

Illustrated by Megan Bair, http://www.mbaircreative.com/

This book is dedicated to every little boy and girl around the world whose hair is just a bit "different".

I've got big hair and I don't care

And even though the kids may stare

I lift my hands up in the air

Then smile and say…

I love my hair!

I've got big hair, my friend does too

And at the movies and the zoo

It often blocks out all the view

So never sit behind us two!

Sometimes I lose at hide and seek

But hair like this is so unique

Braids

Twists

And puffs are all so chic

My hair is different every week

I've got big hair and just for fun

I put my dog's hair in a bun

And then we go out for a run

And laugh and play out in the sun

My hair is big and full of flair

It's like a fancy hat I wear

So sit behind me if you dare

Oh how I really love my hair!

I've got big hair and I'm so proud

It's soft and fluffy like a cloud

And even when it's really loud

You can still find me in a crowd

My hair looks like a cotton ball

And though I'm short it makes me tall

You'll see me walking down the hall

Bookbag and books

Big hair and all

I've got big hair and I don't care

And even though the kids may stare

I lift my hands up in the air

Then smile and say I love my hair!

The End

Made in the USA
San Bernardino, CA
03 June 2020